BIRDS

Diane James & Sara Lynn

Illustrated by Sue Cony

TWO CAN™

PRINCETON ■ LONDON

Fly Like a Bird

Would you like to fly like a bird? There are many different kinds of birds. They all have feathers and wings and most of them can fly.

Birds have beaks instead of mouths and teeth like other animals. They make nests and lay their eggs in them. Baby birds hatch out from the eggs.

WOODPECKERS

Woodpeckers use their sharp beaks to drill holes in tree trunks. They push their long, sticky tongues under the bark to find insects to eat.

Woodpeckers have a clever way of warning other birds to keep out of their territory. They drum on hollow branches with their beaks.

Woodpeckers build their nests inside the holes that they make in trees.

Woodpeckers use their strong tails and feet to help them balance against the trunks of trees.

PARROTS

Parrots live in hot countries. They have bright, colorful feathers.

Most parrots have hooked beaks, which they use to crack open nuts and seeds. They also use their beaks to help them climb trees.

Some parrots lay their eggs in holes in trees. Others lay theirs on the ground or among rocks.

Parrots live together in large groups. They chatter loudly to each other as they perch in the tree tops.

EAGLES

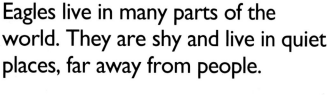

Eagles live in many parts of the world. They are shy and live in quiet places, far away from people.

Eagles soar high up in the sky. They hold their wings out straight when they glide, hardly moving them at all.

Eagles build big nests called eyries. Some eagles live on mountainsides and others nest in tall trees.

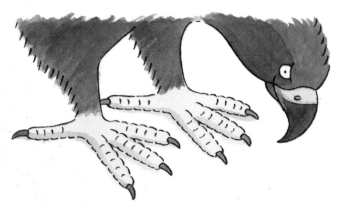

Eagles are hunting birds. They look very fierce with their sharp beaks and claws.

Baby eagles are called eaglets. They are fluffy and weak when they hatch. After about three months, they grow strong enough to leave the nest.

FLAMINGOES

Flamingoes have long, thin necks and legs. Their beaks are big and curved.

Flamingoes often rest by standing on one leg. They fly with their legs stretched out behind them.

Flamingoes make their nests from mounds of mud. The mother lays her egg on the top.

Big flocks of flamingoes usually live together near lakes or marshes.

Flamingoes stretch their beaks down to the water to feed. They scoop out shrimp and other tiny creatures.

SWANS

Swans are large birds. They have long necks and flat beaks. Their legs are short and they have webbed feet.

Baby swans are called cygnets. When they hatch, they are covered in soft grey feathers.

Swans make huge nests on the ground. They build their nests from grass and other plants.

When swans are feeding underwater, they 'up-end' their bodies so that only their feet and tails can be seen.

Small cygnets sometimes ride on their mother's back. This keeps them warm and dry.

OWLS

There are owls living in most parts of the world. They have round, flat faces with huge eyes and hooked beaks.

Owls can turn their heads all the way around to face backwards.

Owls often live in hollow tree trunks or old buildings. The nests they make are rather untidy!

Owls have soft, fluffy feathers which puff out and make them look bigger than they really are.

Owls hunt for their food at night. They usually see better in the dark than in daylight.

PELICANS

Pelicans live by lakes or near the sea. They are good swimmers.

Most pelicans make their nests on the ground, in small hollows. They often nest on islands.

Pelicans have huge, straight beaks. They use the soft pouch underneath to help them hold the fish they catch.

Young pelicans push their heads right into their mother's bill to feed on the fish she has caught.

16

HUMMINGBIRDS

When hummingbirds fly, their wings beat so fast that they are difficult to see. They make a gentle humming sound as they move.

Some hummingbirds are no bigger than a bumble bee. They are the smallest birds in the world.

Hummingbirds are the only birds which can fly backwards.

Hummingbirds use their long beaks and tongues to suck nectar from deep inside flowers.

Hummingbirds build tiny cup-shaped nests. They sometimes take spiders' webs to help stick the nest together.

PENGUINS

Most penguins live in very cold places. They often huddle together to keep warm, taking turns to stand on the outside of the group.

On land, penguins waddle along on their short legs or slide across the ice on their fronts.

Penguins cannot fly. Instead of wings they have flippers, which they use like paddles to help them swim.

Male emperor penguins balance an egg on their feet and cover it with a special fold of skin to keep it warm.

QUIZ

How do young pelicans feed? What do they like to eat?

What do flamingoes use to make their nests?

What do parrots use their hooked beaks for?

When do owls hunt for their food?

Where do eagles live?

What are baby swans called?

How do woodpeckers warn other birds to keep out of their territory?

Which is the smallest bird in the world?

INDEX

Published in the United States and Canada by
Two-Can Publishing LLC
234 Nassau Street
Princeton, NJ 08542

www.two-canpublishing.com

© Two-Can Publishing 2000
Illustration © Sue Cony

For information on Two-Can books and multimedia,
call 1-609-921-6700, fax 1-609-921-3349, or visit our Web site at
http://www.two-canpublishing.com

Created by
act-two
346 Old Street
London EC1V 9RB

Editor: Lucy Duke   Designer: Beth Aves

'Two-Can' is a trademark of Two-Can Publishing.
Two-Can Publishing is a division of Zenith Entertainment plc,
43-45 Dorset Street, London W1H 4AB

ISBN 1-58728-865-6

1 2 3 4 5 6 7 8 9 10 04 03 02 01 00

Photo credits: pp2-3 Oxford Scientific Films, p5 Aquila, p7 Oxford Scientific Films, p9 Oxford Scientific Films,
p11 Bruce Coleman, p13 Ardea, p15 Zefa, p17 The Image Bank, p19 Bruce Coleman, p21 Bruce Coleman

Printed in Hong Kong